Tesla the She[ltie]

in

Doggie Dreams

RACHEL KLEINMAN
& TYLER EMORY

EPIGRAPH BOOKS
RHINEBECK, NEW YORK

Tesla the Sheltie in Doggie Dreams © 2019
by Rachel Kleinman & Tyler Emory

All rights reserved. No part of this book may be used or reproduced in any manner without written permission by the author except in critical articles or reviews. Contact the publisher for information.

ISBN 978-1-948796-74-3

Book design by Rachel Kleinman & Colin Rolfe

Epigraph Books
22 East Market Street, Suite 304
Rhinebeck, NY 12572
(845) 876-4861
EpigraphPS.com

Doggie Dreams

It's bedtime for Tesla,

Zoe turns off the light.

She looks at him and wonders,

"What does my dog dream

about at night?"

I bet when Tesla's hungry
he dreams of pancakes piled high.
Extra butter and syrup,
a stack that reaches the sky!

Tesla enjoys riding in the car

so maybe when he's asleep,

he takes the wheel and with

the wind in his hair—

Look out for Tesla, Beep Beep!

Tesla loves to be pampered,

which means bubble bath

dreams of the tub.

Manicures and duckies,

Rub-a-dub-dub!

A trip to the park
is one of Tesla's favorite things.
Tonight when he closes his eyes,
it's his turn on the swings!

Tesla snuggles with his toys
when he goes to sleep.
Perhaps he dreams of being King,
and ruling a giant toy heap!

When Tesla has a nightmare,
he's being chased around the room.
Because nothing scares Tesla
more than the vacuum!

Maybe Tesla's fantasy

is to someday see the ocean.

A beach chair and a pair of shades—

Do dogs need sunscreen lotion?

"Goodnight, Tesla!
I'm too tired to think of another."
Zoe kissed her pup and patted his head,
and that night they dreamt of each other.

CPSIA information can be obtained
at www.ICGtesting.com
Printed in the USA
BVHW010227250619
551878BV00005B/27/P